Feline Charm

A DAVID FICKLING BOOK

Visit us on the Web! www.randomhouse.com/kids

Educators and librarians, for a variety of teaching tools, visit us at www.randomhouse.com/teachers

Library of Congress Cataloging-in-Publication Data
Wells, Kitty.
Feline charm / Kitty Wells ; [illustrations by Joanna Harrison]. — 1st American ed.
p.   cm. — (Pocket cats)
Summary: The third of Maddy's ceramic cats comes to life to help her best friend Rachel realize her dream of playing the lead in The Nutcracker ballet.
ISBN 978-0-385-75212-1 (trade) — ISBN 978-0-375-89803-7 (ebook)
[1. Cats—Fiction.   2. Magic—Fiction.   3. Ballet dancing—Fiction.
4. Self-confidence—Fiction.]   I. Harrison, Joanna, ill.   II. Title.
PZ7.W46485Fe 2011
[Fic]—dc22
2010038227

Printed in the United States of America
November 2011
10 9 8 7 6 5 4 3 2 1

First American Edition

Feline Charm

Kitty Wells

illustrated by Joanna Harrison

David Fickling Books

OXFORD · NEW YORK

Also by Kitty Wells
Paw Power
Shadow Magic

The *Pocket Cats* series is dedicated to all cat lovers, everywhere . . . including you!

Chapter One

"And *plié* . . . keep your back straight, Poppy . . . much better, Sue."

Madame Dumont walked down the long line of leotard-clad girls, stopping here and there to correct a posture. She had bright red hair piled up on top of her head, and a faint French accent.

Chapter One

Maddy Lloyd stood with one
hand resting on the *barre*, doing the
exercises with the others. Out of the
corner of her eye she could see herself
reflected in the mirrors that lined one
wall: a small girl with a long brown
ponytail, her arm held out gracefully
to one side.

"Nice," said Madame Dumont,
tapping her shoulder as she passed.
Maddy smiled to herself – but her

smile faded as she caught sight of her
best friend, Rachel. The tall blonde
girl's movements were tight and jerky,
and there was an anxious frown on
her face.

Madame Dumont shook her head as
she came to her. "You're still trying
too hard, *ma petite*," she said gently.
"Just let go and feel the music!"

Maddy winced in sympathy at the
glum look on Rachel's face. Poor

Rache – she loved ballet, but no matter how much she practised, she just couldn't seem to relax! She was as stiff as a stick.

"And . . . back to first," Madame instructed them as the music finally came to an end.

Up on her tiptoes, Maddy eased herself down to the floor, sliding her pink-slippered feet into a perfect first position. She sighed happily. She'd been doing ballet for three years now, and enjoyed it hugely. She just wished that Rachel was better at it so that they could both enjoy it together.

With a swirl of long purple skirts, Madame Dumont strode to the front of the studio. "Very good, everyone. And now I have an exciting announcement." Her voice lowered dramatically. "There's going to be a benefit production of *The Nutcracker* at the Civic Auditorium this December – and our ballet school will be taking part!"

An eager murmur swept through the class. Madame Dumont smiled. "Of course, most of the roles will be taken by more advanced dancers, but *The Nutcracker* does have several parts that students in this class can perform . . . including Clara, the main character."

Maddy caught her breath. Clara, the girl who got whisked away on an amazing winter adventure, was just her age.

And though it might be big-headed even to think it, she knew that she was one of the best dancers in her class. She hardly even had to practise; ballet just came naturally to her.

What if . . . what if *she* got the role of Clara?

Poppy Harris's hand shot up. "Madame, will we have to audition?"

Their teacher nodded. "Yes, we'll

be holding auditions this Saturday.
But I still haven't told you the
most exciting part!" Her dark eyes
twinkled. "The role of the Sugarplum
Fairy is going to be danced by a very
fine ballerina . . . Snow Bradley."

A gasp ran through the room.

"*Really*, Madame?"

"I've got her poster on my wall!"

"She was in *Swan Lake*, and
Giselle, and—"

Their teacher laughed. "I see you've
heard of her! Yes, Snow is a former
student of mine. She'll be joining us a
few weeks before the performance."

Maddy was in a daze. She had
a poster of Snow Bradley as well,
dancing in *Romeo and Juliet*. She'd
got the DVD too, and had watched it
more times than she could count. Just

imagine if she got the part of Clara. She'd be dancing with her favourite ballerina ever!

"I've got letters for your parents that will explain everything," Madame was saying. "That's all, girls. Class dismissed."

Her students broke into polite applause and then filed out of the studio to the changing room, chatting eagerly.

"*You'll* get to be Clara, of course," said Rachel, nudging against Maddy's side.

"Definitely – the rest of us won't have a chance," put in Poppy.

Maddy hoped fervently that they were right. She sat down on the bench and started pulling off her shoes to hide her excitement. "Don't be daft,

it could be anyone."

Rachel made a face as she sat down beside her. "Except me, that is."

Maddy bit her lip. She wanted to comfort her friend, but she knew Rachel was right – there was no way she'd be dancing Clara!

Poppy looked uncomfortable too. "Maybe if you practised harder—" she started.

"How could I practise harder?" said Rachel tetchily. "All I ever *do* is practise." Reaching for her bag, she put on her glasses with a sigh. "Anyway, I'd be happy just to take part in the show, so who knows – maybe I'll get lucky at the auditions."

"I hope we *all* get lucky," said Poppy. "Imagine being on the same stage as Snow Bradley – it'd be magic, pure magic!" She did a quick series of pirouettes across the room. The other girls giggled as she bumped into them.

At the word "magic", Maddy and

Rachel exchanged a secret smile.
Though no one else knew it, the two
of them really *had* experienced magic
– in the form of three tiny ceramic
cats. The cats belonged to Maddy, and
could actually come to life – though
so far only two of them had done so.

"Has anything happened with the
third cat yet?" whispered Rachel as
they got changed.

Maddy glanced at the other girls.
They were all talking and laughing,
not paying any attention to them.
Picking up her bag from the corner,
she carefully unzipped the side pocket,
and she and Rachel peeped inside.

The little ceramic set was nestling
in a piece of soft cloth, staring up
at them with painted eyes: a slender
black cat, a chunky grey one, and a

tabby with white markings. It was the
tabby who was due to come to life
this time . . . but he remained as still
and silent as the other two.

Maddy let out a breath, disappointed
despite herself. "I guess it's too soon.
It's only been a few days since Nibs
came to life." She touched the tiny
black cat's smooth head, remembering
the adventure they'd shared.

"I don't think that matters," said Rachel thoughtfully, tying her trainers. "Just because Nibs appeared a few weeks after Greykin, that doesn't mean it will happen the same way again with *this* cat. It could happen any time at all!"

Maddy's scalp tingled as she realized that Rachel was right. Her best friend was very scientific, and often saw a logic in things when Maddy herself did not. It was just as well that Rachel was so awkward at ballet, she reflected. It wouldn't be fair for her to have *all* the talents.

Maddy kept this thought to herself. "I'll let you know the second something happens!" she promised, zipping up the bag again.

"Great," said Rachel happily as she pulled on her jacket. "And maybe *this* time I can find out where the cats came from!"

But the tabby showed no sign of coming to life over the next few days, and Maddy decided she'd been right after all – it was too soon. She still carried the cats in her bag with her, just in case . . . but meanwhile, with

15

the audition coming up, she had other things on her mind too.

Each night Maddy pored over her ballet books, drinking in pictures of Snow Bradley. The famous ballerina was really named Sophia, but everyone called her Snow because of her pale, flaxen hair.

Maddy traced a photo of her up *en pointe*. Snow herself had danced Clara once, when she was first starting out. *Just imagine if I got the part – she could give me tips!* thought Maddy.

Her stomach lurched excitedly. It was Friday night now, and the auditions were the next afternoon. Only a few more hours.

Maddy's mother laughed as she came into the room and spotted Maddy sitting cross-legged on her

bed. "Wouldn't you be better off practising, rather than just staring at your ballet books?" she asked.

Maddy shrugged. She had never practised her ballet very much – somehow she just did well without really trying.

Shaking her head good-naturedly, Maddy's mother dropped a kiss on her forehead. "Time to get ready for bed," she said. "Jack's out of the bath now – and you'll want a good night's sleep before the audition tomorrow."

"OK," agreed Maddy, slowly closing her book.

Later, her hair still slightly damp from her bath, Maddy put on her pyjamas and stared dreamily at herself in the mirror. Rising up on her tiptoes, she

arched her arms gracefully over her head. *As if you're holding a marble between your two middle fingers*, Madame always said.

Maddy's bedroom seemed to fade around her as she began to dance. All at once she wasn't Maddy any more. She was Clara, dressed in her finest clothes at a lavish Christmas party – and she had just been given the most wonderful present ever.

"A nutcracker!" she breathed. She could almost *see* the little wooden man – he was dressed jauntily in red, with a bristling black beard and bright blue eyes.

Maddy spun lightly around the room, pretending to dance with the toy. She was just getting to the part where pesky Fritz, Clara's little brother, grabs the nutcracker and breaks it (Maddy could sympathize: Jack had broken loads of her things in the past) when she heard a soft chuckle.

"Bravo!" called a purring voice. "Bravo!"

Chapter Two

Maddy stumbled in surprise.
Whirling towards her desk, she
saw the tiny cats sitting just where
she'd left them . . . but only two were
still ceramic. The tabby sat on his
haunches with his bushy tail wrapped
neatly about his paws, watching her
with twinkling amber eyes.

"You've come to life!" cried
Maddy. She popped her hand over
her mouth and glanced at the wall.

Jack was in the next room, and it wouldn't do for him to find out about the cats. He couldn't keep a secret for a second.

"Yes – it is I!" announced the cat grandly.

He strolled across the desk, waving his tail from side to side. Stopping near Maddy's eraser, he struck a grand pose. "You may comment on the beauty of my markings if you like," he said. "Don't hold back

for modesty's sake."

Maddy giggled. Sliding into her desk chair, she regarded the little cat with shining eyes. His markings were indeed beautiful. Brown and black stripes swirled across his forehead, back and tail, with pure snowy-white fur covering everywhere else.

"You're gorgeous!" she assured him.

The cat purred with pleasure. "I'm Ollie," he said. "Why haven't you stroked me yet?"

"Sorry," said Maddy with a grin. "I wasn't sure whether you'd want me to." She ran a finger gently over Ollie's back. His long fur was just as soft and silky as it looked.

Ollie blinked. "Wouldn't *want* you to? Why on earth not? My coat is exceedingly luxurious, as you've probably noticed – perfect for stroking!"

"It's lovely," agreed Maddy. She hid a smile as she scratched Ollie's head with her little fingernail. He reminded her of a strutting peacock she had once seen at a wildlife park!

Ollie flopped over onto his back to let Maddy scratch his stomach. "Yes, and it needs regular combing, or I get tangles," he murmured contentedly. "I hope you have a suitable brush."

A *brush*? For a cat five centimetres tall? "Er – I'll find one," promised Maddy.

Finally Ollie got to his feet with a satisfied sigh. "Exquisite," he said. "You have very understanding fingers. Was that *The Nutcracker* you

24

were practising earlier?"

Maddy's eyes widened. "Yes, but – how did you know?" Greykin and Nibs, the two cats she had met before, were each very wise in their different ways, but she was certain neither of them knew much about ballet!

"I have trodden the boards myself in my time," said Ollie with a dramatic sweep of his tail. "You've heard of the Aladdin Theatre, of course?"

Maddy shook her head.

"Oh." Ollie's ears flicked in disappointment. "Well, it was very famous, believe me. The three of us were there for some time, though Nibs and Greykin never quite *embraced* the dramatic life as I did." He gave the other two cats a slightly pitying glance.

"Ah, those were the days," he sighed. "What plays, what characters! Lady Bracknell – Mrs Malaprop – Malvolio!"

Maddy gaped at him. Had the cats *really* been in a theatre? "Mal – who?" she echoed.

"Shakespeare," said Ollie. "*Twelfth Night*." Leaping up onto a library book, he puffed out his furry chest and half yowled, "*Some are born great, some achieve greatness . . . and some have greatness thrust upon them!*"

He gave Maddy an expectant look. She applauded softly, and he dipped his head in thanks. "So you see, my dear, I know a bit about the theatre . . . and as for ballet, we always performed *The Nutcracker* at

Christmas. Along with a good panto, of course."

Maddy wished fervently that Rachel were here. None of the cats had ever volunteered so much about their past before – she hardly knew where to begin with her questions!

"Ollie, where was the—" she started.

"May I have a tour?" interrupted Ollie, jumping down from the book. He padded across the desk and nudged her hand with his head.

"I see you have a most charming room. Pink and yellow; very sweet."

"Oh – of course." Distracted for a moment, Maddy turned her hand over and felt Ollie's slight furry weight as he stepped onto her palm. Happiness fluttered through her. She'd never get tired of having tiny magical cats – and Ollie really *was*

a very beautiful one.

Maddy rose from her chair, and then remembered her question. "Ollie, was the theatre in London, or—"

"And *who* is that beautiful ballerina on the wall?" demanded Ollie, craning his head for a better look.

He meant her poster of Snow Bradley! Maddy forgot her interest in Ollie's past as she eagerly told him all about the famous ballerina, even getting out her ballet books to show him other photos.

"If I'm not mistaken, I think the problem we need to solve might involve her," said Ollie thoughtfully.

Maddy was sitting cross-legged on her bed by then, with the little cat perched on her knee. "The problem is with *Snow Bradley*?" she gasped.

The cats only came to life when there was some sort of trouble that needed their attention, but Maddy had never dreamed that it might involve her favourite ballerina!

With a quick spring, Ollie landed on the book. He gazed down at a glossy photo of Snow leaping through the air in a *grand jeté*.

"Yes, I think so," he said. "It's not *directly* about her, but I'm definitely

getting a sort of pre-tingling sensation in my whiskers. They're very sensitive, you know, as well as being extremely long and elegant."

"*Wow*," breathed Maddy. Was she going to be able to help Snow in some way? She opened her mouth to ask – and then jumped as her bedroom door opened and her mother came in.

"Maddy! Aren't you in bed yet?"

Sitting on the open page of the book, Ollie was now just a ceramic cat again. Mum picked him up and placed him back on Maddy's desk with a tiny *clink*.

"Come on, sweetie, into bed – you've got a big day tomorrow!"

Maddy blinked. She had forgotten about the

audition! "OK," she said quickly, climbing under the covers.

Her mother kissed her and turned out the light. Maddy lay listening until her footsteps faded away down the landing – and then she quietly slipped out of bed, lit by the glow of her pink fairy nightlight.

"Oh Juliet, wherefore art thou?" whispered a feline voice.

Maddy giggled. She could just make out Ollie's amber eyes in the faint light. "Here," she whispered back, going over to the desk.

He leaped onto her hand with a flourish of his tail. "Did you see how quickly I changed back to ceramic?" he bragged, rubbing against her thumb. "Lightning reflexes! I've never been caught yet."

Maddy didn't think the other two cats had ever been caught either, but she didn't point this out. "Where would you like to sleep?" she asked. "Greykin slept in my jewellery box, and Nibs—"

Ollie stopped rubbing and looked surprised. "Why, with you, of course."

"Me?" echoed Maddy. "But—"

Ollie's voice was firm. "Yes – where else? I only sleep on pillows; anything else musses up my fur. Besides, I want to be close to you."

A delicious warmth spread through Maddy at the thought of the tiny cat curling up next to her – but then she realized there was a problem. "But, Ollie, what if I roll over onto you during the night?" she whispered. "I'd squash you flat!"

Feline Charm

"You won't,"
Ollie assured her.
"My magic comes
in very helpful at
times like these."

"What *is* your
magic?" whispered
Maddy eagerly as
she carried Ollie
over to the bed.
Each of the cats
had a different magical power, which
they could also give to her. So far,
Maddy had enjoyed a cat's physical
prowess and the ability to become
almost invisible – she couldn't
imagine what Ollie's power might be!

But Ollie shook his striped head.
"I couldn't possibly tell you yet.
Haven't you ever heard of dramatic

exposition? One must always hold back until the perfect moment."

Though Maddy wasn't sure what "dramatic exposition" was, Ollie's meaning was clear enough: he wasn't going to tell her until he was good and ready. "Just a hint?" she suggested as she slipped back under the covers.

The tiny tabby leaped onto the pillow beside her head. "A hint . . ." he purred thoughtfully. "Yes, that could even *add* to the drama, couldn't it? All right, then – it's not what people think it is!"

"But that could mean anything at all," protested Maddy.

Ollie didn't answer. Settling down beside Maddy's ear, he carefully arranged himself into a perfect fluffy circle. "This is a lovely pillow,"

he murmured.
"It shows off
my markings
beautifully."

"Well, at least
tell me more about the Aladdin
Theatre," whispered Maddy. "Was it
in London? What were you and the
other cats doing there?"

The only answer was a faint feline
snore in her ear. Maddy sighed,
though she wasn't really surprised.
She knew from experience that the
cats never told her anything unless
they felt like it!

Stroking Ollie's silky back with one
finger, Maddy closed her eyes and
drifted into a lovely daydream. She
was on stage at the Civic Auditorium
with Snow Bradley, and the audience

was cheering them wildly, stamping and shouting, *"Encore! Encore!"*

Then the famous ballerina held up her hands for silence. *"Please, everyone, I must say thank you to Maddy Lloyd . . . without her help, I could not have danced the Sugarplum Fairy the way this part truly deserves . . ."*

Maddy smiled as she floated off to sleep, one finger still on Ollie's softly rising sides. She could hardly wait for the auditions tomorrow. She just knew she was going to dance better than she'd ever danced before!

Chapter Three

The next afternoon Maddy's mum dropped her off in front of the Dumont Ballet Studio. "Break a leg, sweetie," she said as Maddy got out of the car.

"Break a *leg*?" hooted Jack from the back seat. "Then she'd be on crutches and couldn't dance!"

Mum laughed. "It's just theatre people's way of saying 'good luck'," she explained. "Bye, Maddy – we're

going to the library, and then I'll be
back for you around four o'clock."

Maddy waved as her mother drove
away, with Jack pulling faces at her
from the back window. She didn't
make a face back. Girls who hoped to
dance in *The Nutcracker* with Snow
Bradley were far too grown up to do
such a thing!

Most of the other girls were already
in the changing room, putting on
their ballet slippers or adjusting their
leotards.

"Oh, Maddy, I'm
so glad you're here,"
moaned Rachel.
She was sitting
on the bench,
looking pale.
"I'm so nervous
– I just know
I'm going to
be terrible."

"You won't be," Maddy assured
her. She carefully put down her bag.
Ollie was snuggled into one of its side
pockets, on a pillow she'd made for
him out of a silk handkerchief, and
she was dying to tell Rachel about him.

Feline Charm

"Oh yes I will," said Rachel
gloomily. She slumped, with her chin
in her hands. "I'm fine on my own,
but whenever I try to dance in front of
someone else I go all stiff and clumsy.
It's *awful*. I don't even know why I
bothered coming."

Quickly pulling on her ballet things,
Maddy drew her friend to one side.
"Rachel, listen," she
whispered. "It's
happened again!"

Rachel's eyes
widened. "The
tabby!" she cried.
"Oh, brilliant!
What's he called?"

But before
Maddy could answer, Madame
Dumont appeared at the door.

"Time to get started, girls."

Suddenly Maddy remembered that Ollie had asked to be near the auditions, in case the problem had something to do with them. But they weren't supposed to take their bags into the studio – and her ballet outfit was tights and a leotard, with no pockets in sight.

The other girls were already filing out. "Madame, may I bring my cat figurine along, for luck?" blurted Maddy.

She took the ceramic Ollie out of her bag, and then bit back a smile. The little cat had frozen in a dance pose, up on his hind legs with his nose in the air!

Madame Dumont chuckled. "A ballet cat! Yes, I suppose so. He can sit on the piano – perhaps he will bring good luck to the other girls too."

Following Madame into the studio, Maddy carefully placed Ollie on the gleaming black surface of the grand piano. It was so shiny that she could see a second Ollie reflected at his feet. She hurried to join the other girls at the *barre*.

"You brought the cat!" whispered Rachel.

Before Maddy could respond, Madame clapped her hands for attention. "We shall begin with some warm-up exercises," she told them.

Once they'd done the warm-ups, their teacher divided them into smaller groups. "Now, I shall just teach you the first part of Clara's dance. Arms out like this . . ."

Miss Henry began to play the piano, and Maddy almost forgot that she was in the old familiar studio surrounded by other girls in leotards. Just like before in her bedroom, she was Clara again, dancing at an exciting Christmas party.

Thump! The noise echoed around the studio as Rachel tripped over her own feet. Everyone turned to stare at her. "Sorry," she muttered, red-faced.

"All right, let me see each of you on your own," said Madame Dumont after a while. "Rachel, would you go first, please?"

Slowly Rachel walked to the front of the studio and took up the position. Her mouth was tight, as if she were concentrating hard. Maddy watched anxiously, willing her friend to do well.

The music began and Rachel started to dance, moving jerkily. Though she knew all the steps, she was so rigid she looked like a robot. The class held back giggles as Rachel's arms flapped instead of fluttered, and Maddy bit her lip. Oh, poor Rachel!

Madame Dumont motioned for Miss Henry to stop. Putting a hand on Rachel's shoulder, she said, "Relax, *ma petite*! It's not a maths problem – you need to let go and *feel*."

Rachel scowled so ferociously
that Maddy knew she was struggling
against tears. "Yes, Madame," she
mumbled.

But her dancing was no better when
she started again. In fact, Maddy
thought, it was even worse! Rachel
knew it too. Her face was bright red
as she moved stiffly through the
steps.

"All right, thank you, Rachel," said
Madame gently. "Let me see someone

else now. Sue, would you do the
dance for us?"

Rachel slunk back to the other
girls as Sue went to the front. "I wish
I'd never come," she whispered in
Maddy's ear. "I must have looked like
an idiot!"

Maddy didn't know what to say.
"You weren't all *that* bad," she
murmured back weakly as the music
began. Rachel made a
face and didn't
answer.

Finally it was
Maddy's turn. Though
she was worried about
Rachel, her heartbeat
quickened as she went
to the front of the studio.
Sliding her feet into fifth

position, she stood up straight, with one arm curved in front of her and the other arching above her head.

The music began, and Maddy plunged into the Christmas dance, skipping lightly about the room. Distantly she was aware of the other girls, and of Ollie still sitting on top of the piano – but mostly she was just Clara, dancing at her parents' party.

"Very good, Maddy. With a bit of work, that would be excellent," said Madame when the music ended. "Poppy, would you go now?"

Still tingling with excitement, Maddy joined the other girls.

"You looked wonderful, Maddy," whispered Rachel, trying to smile. "I just know you're going to be Clara."

When the auditions were over, it

was almost four o'clock. As the other girls headed for the changing room, Maddy went to the piano to collect Ollie – and stopped short with a gasp. The little cat had come to life again, and was sitting up on the piano, waving his tail to catch her attention!

Miss Henry was busy putting away her sheet music and hadn't seen him. Maddy quickly scooped Ollie up, and then bit back a startled squawk as he leaped onto her shoulder in a white and brown blur, clinging to her leotard with his claws.

"I know what the problem is!" he hissed in her ear. "It's that friend of

yours, the tall blonde girl – we have
to—"

"Maddy? What are you doing?"
asked Miss Henry, looking up.

"Er – nothing," stammered Maddy.
Ollie had turned into a ceramic cat
again, and she only just managed to
grab him before he tumbled off her
shoulder onto the polished wooden
floor.

Her pulse pounded as she hurried
into the changing room with Ollie
cupped safely in her hands. The
problem was *Rachel*? But what on
earth was wrong?

Rachel had already changed into her
jeans, and was sitting on the bench
tying her trainers. To Maddy's relief,
she didn't ask about Ollie again. In
fact, she still looked rather glum.

"I've got to go," she said, picking up her bag. "Mum said she'd be here at four o'clock on the dot."

"Oh," said Maddy in surprise. "Well, if you just wait a second, I'll be ready too—"

Rachel took a step back. "No, I'd better hurry. See you at school, Maddy. And – and you did really well, you know!" Ducking her head down, she rushed out of the room.

Poppy raised her eyebrows knowingly. "She's in a strop because she did so badly."

"Rachel doesn't get into strops," protested Maddy. "She's just upset, that's all."

"I'd be upset too," put in a girl called Freya. "She was really awful, wasn't she? It's weird that

she's so bad when she practises so much."

Maddy wanted to say something sharp, but Freya wasn't being nasty – in fact, she looked as if she felt sorry for Rachel.

"Anyway, *you* were great, Maddy," said Poppy. "You're going to be Clara for sure, I just know it!"

"Thanks," she muttered. For some reason, this didn't make her feel very good. Tucking Ollie back into her bag, Maddy quickly got changed and rushed outside, hoping to catch her friend – but Rachel's mum's car was just driving away.

As Maddy stood staring after it, her own mother pulled up. "How did you do?" she asked cheerfully as Maddy got in.

"Oh – OK, I think," said Maddy.

In the back seat, Jack was wearing a mask made of bright green paper. "There was a spaceship day at the library!" he cried. "Look, Maddy, we all made alien masks."

"Great," said Maddy. Her bag sat nestled against her feet. She felt cold as she gazed down at it. She couldn't imagine what the problem with Rachel might be.

What was Ollie going to tell her when she managed to get him alone?

Chapter Four

The moment Maddy got home, she rushed up to her room and took Ollie out of her bag. He came to life immediately, sitting on her palm and swishing his long bushy tail back and forth.

"Ollie, what's wrong with Rachel?" whispered Maddy. "I thought you said the problem was to do with Snow Bradley!"

He shook his head. "Not directly –

though Snow Bradley is somehow involved. No, the problem is that your friend's about to give up ballet."

"Oh, no!" cried Maddy. She sat down on her bed with a *thump*. "But Rachel *loves* ballet! She mustn't stop, she really mustn't."

"Yes, it would be a terrible mistake," said the little cat. "Fortunately there is a solution!" He drew himself up proudly. "Rachel needs to perform in *The Nutcracker* so that she realizes how good she can be."

"*Rachel?*" repeated Maddy dumbly. "But – we've already had the auditions! And besides, Ollie, you saw her. She was really, really bad."

"She was nervous," corrected Ollie, leaping across to her bedside table. He

perched on
top of her
clock and
twitched his
whiskers
knowingly.
"Stage
fright; I've
seen it a
hundred

times. But your power should do the
trick – and I'm sure it can arrange
another audition for her, as well."

"What *is* my power?" asked Maddy,
leaning forward.

Ollie didn't answer. He sat up
straight, his amber eyes fixed upon
her. They seemed to grow larger
and larger, and all at once a thought
popped into her head – *Ollie's brush!*

He had asked her to get him one, and she still hadn't done it. Suddenly it seemed very urgent. Maddy jumped to her feet. "I'll be right back," she said in a rush. "I've got to go and find—"

"Sit down," Ollie laughed. "I was merely giving you a demonstration. *That* is your power – a bit of feline persuasion! Haven't you ever wondered why humans are always opening doors for us cats, or letting us sleep on the best part of the bed?"

Maddy's jaw dropped open. "You mean – cats have *mind control*?"

"More like mind *suggestion*," said Ollie smugly. "We can't get someone to do something against their will, or something that they believe is wrong. But we *can* put an idea in someone's head that they'll assume is their own – and more often than not, they'll act on it!"

"Wow," whispered Maddy. And now this was *her* power too. The thought of being able to plant ideas in people's heads was quite dizzying. Imagine what she could do with such a power at school!

"That's what my hint meant, you see," explained Ollie. "*It's not what people think it is* – they might *think* they're having their own thoughts, but they're not! Wasn't that clever of me?"

Privately Maddy didn't think it had been a very good clue at all, but she

didn't say so. "So I can make Rachel
feel more confident, and then she'll
dance better?" she asked eagerly.

"Well, that's the plan." Ollie began
washing his tail, attacking it with
long strokes of his tongue. "But
it's not an exact science, I'm afraid
– you humans aren't always very
predictable."

"Oh," said Maddy. She bit her
thumb. "How can we be sure it's
going to work, then?"

Ollie looked up and smiled.
"Simple," he purred. "Practise!"

"*Pow!*" cried Jack, leaping off the
sofa. "I'm an alien from planet
Murgatroyd!" His paper mask had
tentacles drawn on it, and fangs
hanging from its mouth.

Maddy sat curled up on an armchair in the lounge, pretending to read a book as she watched her little brother charge about the room, waving his plastic light sabre. He had brought all his space toys down from his bedroom, and the lounge was littered with them.

"Calm down, Jack!" called Mum from the kitchen. "It's almost time for dinner."

Dad appeared in his study doorway. "Yes, let's pick up some of this mess now, Jack."

"I'm not Jack!" he bellowed, leaping onto the sofa again. "I'm an alien!"

Maddy grinned to herself. Her little brother got into these wild moods sometimes, and talking reasonably to him never helped – though her parents never gave up!

Reaching into her pocket, Maddy felt Ollie's ceramic coolness and remembered what he had told her.

First, feel the cat magic flowing through you. Then look at the person you're giving the suggestion to and think it loudly

at them, like shouting in your head!

"That's *enough*, Jack," snapped Dad, snatching him off the sofa. "Come on, let's tidy this mess."

"No!" Jack wriggled like a fish, kicking his legs.

"Jack . . ." said Dad warningly.

"I'm an alien! I'll zap you!"

With a shiver, Ollie came to life in Maddy's pocket and nudged her finger. Shutting her eyes briefly, she felt the feline magic sweep through her, like electricity tickling every pore. Then she opened her eyes and looked right at Jack, still squirming in Dad's grasp.

DO WHAT MUM AND DAD TELL YOU! she shouted in her mind. *BE REALLY, REALLY GOOD! THAT'S AN ORDER!*

Abruptly Jack went limp, his eyes wide.

"Jack?" Dad put him on the ground again.

Jack stood with his mouth hanging open. Maddy watched him nervously. Had she overdone it?

Then, all at once, Jack shook his head and came to life. "Come on, Dad, it's time to tidy up now," he said, pulling off his alien mask. "Would you put this somewhere safe for me, please? I wouldn't want to mess it up."

"Er . . . all right," said Dad, accepting the mask. "Are you feeling OK, Jack? You didn't hit your head on anything when you were jumping about, did you?"

"No, I'm fine." Jack marched

about the room, picking up his toys. "Do you think I have time to get the hoover out before dinner? I wouldn't want Mum to have to do it later."

Wiping her hands on a tea towel, Mum came into the lounge and stared at her son as he passed by, carrying his toys. "Why, Jack, thank you," she said in surprise.

"He wants to get the hoover out," said Dad in an undertone. "Jenny, do you think he's ill?"

Maddy bit her lip to keep from bursting into giggles. There was a banging noise from the cupboard under the stairs, and then Jack reappeared, dragging the hoover.

"I'll just be a minute, Mum," he said cheerfully as he plugged it in. "Dinner smells great."

Mum
put her hand on his forehead with a
frown. "Jack, do you feel all right?"

"I'm fine!" He started up the
hoover, raising his voice over its roar.
"I just thought I'd be really, really
good, that's all."

"Oh." Mum stared at Dad, who
gave a helpless shrug. "Well . . . thank
you."

The spell continued during dinner.

"May I have lots
of vegetables,
please?" asked Jack,
holding out his plate.
"Especially broccoli. It's really good
for me."

"But you hate broccoli," said Mum
weakly, spooning some onto his plate.

"Yes, but vegetables are important,"
said Jack. He started busily cutting up
the green spears. "You and Dad are
always saying so."

Dad rubbed his beard. "The
worrying thing is, I don't think he's
having us on," he muttered to Mum.
"It's like he's had a personality
transplant."

Or a cat spell, thought Maddy,
sneaking a tiny scrap of pork chop
to Ollie in her pocket. She was

beginning to feel a bit concerned.
What if the magic was permanent? It
would be awful to have such a goody-
two-shoes for a brother – he'd show
her up without even trying!

Then she had an idea. The whole
point was for her to get some practice,
wasn't it? So why shouldn't she
change Jack back again?

She gently tapped Ollie. The little
cat seemed to understand. He touched
her finger with his cool nose in
response, and Maddy felt the magic
rush through her once more, like a
fizzy drink in her veins.

BE YOURSELF AGAIN! she
shouted silently at her little brother.
GO BACK TO NORMAL!

Jack froze with his fork midway
to his mouth . . . and then came back

to himself with a shiver. He gaped down at the broccoli. The surprise on his face was so comical that Maddy had to pop a hand over her mouth to stop herself laughing. Fortunately her parents were both staring at Jack!

"*BLEURGH!*" he said, dropping his fork with a clatter. "What am I *doing*? I hate broccoli!"

Feline Charm

Maddy's parents relaxed with twin sighs of relief. "Pick up your fork and don't be rude," said Mum happily. "Here, Jack, have some more mash instead." She heaped a big spoonful onto his plate.

"Yes, and then maybe later we'll have a good old messy game of something!" put in Dad.

Jack gave Maddy a look that said, *Have they gone mad, or what?* She smiled at him and shrugged.

After dinner, Maddy returned to her bedroom and took Ollie out of her pocket. "The magic really works!" she exclaimed.

"Of course it does," said Ollie, preening himself on her palm. "And, as you've seen, it can be

73

very powerful – so you need to be careful what suggestion you make to someone."

"I will," promised Maddy. There wasn't any school on Monday because of a teacher training day, so she'd have to wait until ballet class on Monday afternoon to use the magic on Rachel.

She smiled to herself, imagining it. Since she'd first started to use the feline magic, this was one time she didn't see how anything could possibly go wrong!

But when Monday afternoon came, a troubling thought occurred to Maddy. "Ollie, what if Rachel doesn't go?" she said, taking a clean leotard from her drawer.

Feline Charm

"Mm?" Ollie was sitting on the chest of drawers, admiring himself in the oval mirror. She'd groomed him for almost an hour earlier, with a tiny brush she'd found on the end of one of Mum's eyebrow pencils, and his fur was looking particularly soft and fluffy.

"Because she said that she'd see me at *school*, remember?" continued Maddy, tucking the leotard in her bag. "But she knew we didn't have school today. So what if she's already decided to stop ballet, and won't be back again?"

Ollie frowned. "Yes, that's a point. We'd better use the magic on her now, to get her to come to the class."

"*Can* we?" breathed Maddy. Somehow this seemed far more magical than using the power on someone who was standing right next to her.

"It's not as effective, but it sometimes does the trick. Let us *take arms against a sea of troubles!*" said Ollie, striking a heroic pose.

Maddy blinked. "Do what?"

Feline Charm

"*Hamlet*. We can but try," explained Ollie. With a final loving glance at himself in the mirror, he padded across the chest of drawers to Maddy's hand. "Touch my fur and think of Rachel," he instructed. "See her really clearly in your mind – every freckle, every hair."

Remembering how touching Greykin's fur had once made her visualize the school bully clearly too, Maddy closed her eyes and rested a finger on Ollie's striped back. Immediately an image of

Rachel popped into her head. Maddy could see her best friend's long blonde hair pulled back in a slightly messy ponytail, her glasses perched on top of her nose, her bright blue eyes.

"Now – give her the suggestion!" said Ollie. ·

Maddy's face screwed up as she shouted in her mind: *COME TO BALLET CLASS! YOU REALLY, REALLY WANT TO COME TO BALLET CLASS THIS AFTERNOON!*

The Rachel in her mind didn't react. Maddy thought the words at her a few more times for good measure, and then opened her eyes. "I don't know whether that worked or not," she said doubtfully.

"Only one way to find out . . ." said Ollie, rubbing his head against her

78

finger. "And now, if you'd be so kind – I think you might have *just* enough time to groom me again before we leave!"

Chapter Five

Maddy's mother dropped her off at ballet class a bit earlier than usual, so that she could do some shopping. The moment Maddy walked into the changing room, she was glad of it – because there sat Rachel, already dressed in her leotard!

"You came!" burst out Maddy. None of the other girls had arrived yet, so it was just the two of them in the small room.

Feline Charm

Rachel's cheeks turned pink. She traced a slipper-clad toe on the floor. "Um . . . so you guessed I wasn't going to come back, then, after my awful audition."

"But you *did* come back," said Maddy happily. Placing her bag with Ollie in it on the bench, she started changing into her own ballet things.

Rachel frowned. "Yes, it was pretty weird, actually. I had already told Mum that – that I didn't want to do ballet any more. And then, about half an hour ago . . ." She shook her head in confusion. "I don't know – suddenly I just really felt like coming."

"Weird," agreed Maddy. She moved on quickly in case Rachel started asking awkward questions. "I'm *so* glad you came, though. You can't give up ballet, Rache. You know how much you love it!"

Rachel sighed and played with the elastic band of her ballet slipper. "I don't love looking so stupid, though. Maddy, it's awful. I know how to do the steps, but I just can't! I freeze up."

Madame Dumont came into the

changing room from the studio. "I *thought* I heard voices in here," she said with a smile. "You two are early."

Suddenly Maddy realized that this was her perfect chance, before class started! She closed her eyes, willing Ollie to send her the cat magic. Immediately the prickling feeling swept through her, from her slippers all the way up to her ponytail.

Opening her eyes again, Maddy gazed at Madame Dumont. *LET RACHEL AUDITION AGAIN!* she shouted in her mind.

The ballet teacher started slightly, as if someone had pricked her with a pin. "Rachel, would

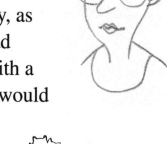

you—?" she began, and then stopped, her red eyebrows drawn together in confusion.

"What, Madame?" asked Rachel.

Their teacher slowly shook her head. "Never mind. It was just a thought."

GIVE RACHEL ANOTHER CHANCE, PLEASE PLEASE PLEASE! shouted Maddy, even louder this time.

Madame Dumont straightened decisively. "Rachel, I am going to give you another chance!" she announced. "Would you like to audition again?"

Rachel's eyes widened. "*What?* I mean – Madame, how could I? I've already auditioned—"

"Yes, but you weren't really

84

dancing your best, were you?" said Madame. "I know you can do better than that, Rachel. Come along now, before the others get here. We shall see what you can do!"

She strode away into the studio, where Maddy could hear her giving instructions to Miss Henry at the piano. Rachel looked as pale as snow. "What am I going to do?" she hissed, grabbing Maddy's arm. "I don't *want* to audition again. I did badly enough the first time!"

The cat magic was still tingling through Maddy. Without answering her friend out loud, she thought, *DO IT! YOU'RE NOT NERVOUS AT ALL! YOU'LL DANCE REALLY, REALLY WELL!*

Rachel jumped. "Did you say something?" she gasped. "It sounded like—"

"Me? No," said Maddy innocently. "But why not just give it a go, Rachel?"

The colour was returning to Rachel's face. "Maybe I will," she said suddenly. "I – I don't really feel nervous any more. You know what, Maddy – maybe it would even be fun!"

Without waiting for Maddy's response, Rachel pushed through the swing doors into the studio. Maddy slipped after her and stood against the wall, watching.

Rachel went to the centre of the

room and took up the position, her
arms curved. Maddy could already
see a difference. Her friend seemed
relaxed and confident, instead of
looking as if she expected someone to
drop an anvil on her head!

"Now begin," said Madame.

As Miss Henry started to play,
Rachel leaped into the dance. There
was a wide smile on her face, and her
movements were feather-light as she
skipped and spun about the studio.

Maddy slowly straightened up

from the wall, staring. Was this really
Rachel? But – she was wonderful!
She had practised so much that her
movements had a tight precision
to them, and now that she wasn't
nervous any more, there was a real
fire and passion to her dancing as
well.

In fact . . . Maddy swallowed. In
fact, Rachel was even better than she
was.

There was a whispering noise
behind her. Turning, Maddy saw
that the other girls had arrived, and
were gaping through the window in
amazement.

The music ended and Rachel's
dance ended with it, perfectly on the
beat. She held the pose for a moment,
arms above her head, and then dipped

into a low curtsy.

Applause burst out from the changing room. The girls rushed in, swarming over Rachel like excited puppies. "That was *wonderful!*" gasped Poppy. "Wow, you've really got better!"

"You certainly have!" agreed Madame warmly. "I am most impressed, *ma petite*. Now, I must just go and change something. Please, girls, start warming up." Her skirts swirled about her ankles as she strode off towards her office.

Rachel was smiling as if she'd never be able to stop. "Maddy, did you see me?" she cried, bouncing over to her. "I did it, I really *did* it!"

Suddenly Maddy felt awful for her moment of jealousy. Rachel had been

trying so hard
for ages – she
should be happy
for her. "You
were fantastic!"
she said, squeezing
Rachel's arm. "You'll get to be in the
show now for sure."

"Gosh, yes," said Sue. "In fact, I
bet . . ." She trailed off, looking from
Maddy to Rachel and back again.

Cold prickles swept over Maddy.
Sue couldn't mean that Rachel might
get Clara instead of her, could she?

"The *barre*, girls," called Miss
Henry.

Taking her place, Maddy woodenly
began the warm-up exercises. No,
it was impossible. Rachel would be
in the show, of course, but Madame

couldn't give her the part of Clara. She just couldn't!

When Madame entered the studio again, she was holding a sheet of paper. "Now then," she said, motioning for them to stop. "I know you must all be anxious to hear the results of the auditions."

Maddy's hand slipped off the *barre*. She stood very still, her heart pounding.

Feline Charm

"I must admit to being surprised," said Madame, smiling at Rachel. "But, Rachel, all your practising has finally paid off – that was quite the loveliest dancing that I've seen in a long time. I would like you to dance the role of Clara."

No! Maddy felt as if Madame had just thrown a bucket of cold water over her. Rachel looked stunned as well. "*Me?*" she gasped.

Madame nodded. "Yes, my dear, and I think you will do wonderfully, so long as you don't get nervous."

"Oh, I won't," breathed Rachel. "Honestly, Madame – I feel like I could never ever be nervous about dancing again!"

No, because I'm helping you out with cat magic, thought Maddy. The least Rachel could do was give her a sympathetic look! But her eyes were shining as if she'd forgotten all about her best friend.

"Now then, the other roles," said Madame, consulting her sheet. "Maddy, I would like you to be Rachel's understudy. This is very important, in case Rachel can't dance for any reason."

Rachel did give her a look now, biting her lip anxiously. Maddy somehow managed to smile as if she were delighted with this news.

Distantly she heard Madame continue: "I would also like you to dance as one

94

of King Rat's mouse minions. Now,
Poppy . . ."

A mouse minion. Maddy felt close
to tears. The worst thing was that she
had been Clara, she just knew it. That
was what Madame had had to go and
change, crossing Maddy's name off
the list and adding Rachel's to it!

When Madame had finished
announcing all the parts, she began
class as usual. Maddy danced in a
daze, trying to hide how awful she
felt. Rachel was still dancing better
than any of them, moving gracefully
through the steps.

The moment class was over, Maddy
hurried back to the changing room.
Behind her, she could hear the other
girls congratulating Rachel. When
Rachel came in, her happy smile

faded to a look of concern.

"Maddy?" she said, coming over to her. "You – you're not cross, are you?"

"Of course not!" said Maddy, putting on a bright smile. "I'm really pleased for you."

"Really?" said Rachel, her blue eyes wide and hopeful.

"Of course! You've worked so hard, and – and you really deserve this." Maddy's voice came out thin and strained. She knew that she *should* be pleased for her friend, but how could she be?

Rachel gave her a keen look, as if trying to work out whether Maddy meant what she said or not. "But aren't you disappointed that *you're* not Clara?"

Maddy shrugged, looking away as she undid her ponytail. "Maybe a little. But we'll have lots of fun being in the show together – that's the important thing."

Rachel's face lit up. "It is, isn't it? Oh, Maddy, I'm *so* glad you're not upset. I can hardly believe it – I'm going to be dancing with Snow Bradley! I can't wait to tell my parents – they'll be so surprised . . ."

Maddy's smile felt plastered onto her face as Rachel jabbered on and on. Finally Rachel noticed that she wasn't saying anything. "Maddy, are you *sure* you're OK?" she asked again.

Maddy pulled on her jacket. "Yes, positive."

Rachel looked uncertain, but didn't pursue it. "Well – what about the third cat?" she asked, lowering her voice. "You said he'd come to life. Tell me all about him!"

A small, nasty part of Maddy wanted to tell Rachel exactly what the problem had been. But she couldn't; that would be mean. "No, I – I was just making it up," she faltered.

Rachel stared at her. "Making it up?"

Maddy swung her bag over her

shoulder. "Yes, to cheer you up, because you were so nervous. I thought it would take your mind off things."

Rachel seemed lost for words. Finally she shook her blonde head. "Well . . . thanks, I guess. But, Maddy, it really seemed like—"

"I've got to go; Mum's probably here," broke in Maddy, backing away a step. "See you at school tomorrow,

Rachel. And – and well done, getting Clara! I'm really happy for you."

And before her friend could answer, Maddy fled from the changing room, fighting the tears.

Chapter Six

O n the way home Maddy suddenly realized that things were even worse than she had thought. Now that the problem was sorted, Ollie would be leaving.

Her throat felt tight as she slumped against the seat of the car, holding her bag to her chest. It wasn't fair. She had only known Ollie for a few days, and now it might be ages and ages before he came to life again!

Her mother touched her shoulder as she parked in their drive. "I *am* sorry that you didn't get Clara, sweetie," she said. "But how lovely for Rachel! And you two will have lots of fun dancing together."

"I know," muttered Maddy. She wished her mother hadn't said anything.

As soon as they got inside, Maddy headed up to her room and shut the door. Her fingers shook slightly as she unzipped the side pocket of her bag. She had an awful feeling that Ollie would already be ceramic again, and that she'd find him cold and stiff.

But he was as alive as ever, blinking up at her from his pillow.

Maddy's shoulders sagged with relief. "You're still here!"

Ollie winked at her. "Trying to get rid of me already?" he asked, leaping out of the bag onto her arm.

Maddy stroked his long fur with a finger. "No, of course not! Only – only I thought the problem would be solved, now that Rachel's got a part in *The Nutcracker*."

She tried to keep the resentful tone from her voice, but she didn't succeed. "Oh, Ollie, why did she have to get Clara?" she burst out. "*I* was supposed to get it!"

The little cat gave her a sympathetic look. "The magic doesn't usually make mistakes like that," he said gently. "Things have worked out the way they were supposed to, Maddy."

"Oh," said Maddy in a tiny voice.

"Never mind," said Ollie, rubbing against her thumb. "There are no small parts, only small actors! Dance your heart out in your given role, that's what I say."

Maddy sighed. Of course she would, but it still wouldn't be nearly as good as dancing Clara. "So . . . you don't have to go yet?" she ventured, stroking Ollie's beautiful tail.

He shook his head. "Not yet. Rachel's only got the part; she hasn't

performed it in front of an audience
yet. The problem won't be truly
solved until then."

Maddy's pulse quickened as she
gazed at the miniature cat in her hand.
"You mean – you're staying until the
show opens?" she gasped, lifting him
up to eye level. "But that's brilliant!
That's *weeks* away!"

Ollie patted her nose
with a tiny paw. "Yes,
I'm afraid you're
stuck with me," he
said cheerfully.
"I don't mind."
She grinned.
"Oh, Ollie,
that's wonderful –
it even makes up for not being Clara."
Then Maddy caught sight of her
poster of Snow Bradley, looking pale
and beautiful as she danced *en pointe*
as Juliet. She bit her lip. Well, maybe
it didn't *quite* make up for it . . . but it
certainly made it a lot easier to bear.

As the days passed, Maddy thought
gloomily that if it hadn't been for
Ollie, she might have been tempted

to give up ballet herself. All they did in class now was rehearse for *The Nutcracker*. And no matter how often Maddy told herself that the magic had got things right, she couldn't help it – seeing Rachel twirl lightly through Clara's steps gave her a hard, tight feeling in her chest.

"Maddy, are you *sure* you're not cross with me?" pressed Rachel at school. She adjusted her glasses on her nose. "You seem so . . . quiet all the time now."

"I'm sure," said Maddy, forcing a smile. It was break time, and they were standing outside in the chilly playground. "Come on, let's go and grab the swings before Sherry gets them!"

She set off at a run, and was soon

swinging so high that conversation was impossible. Rachel swung beside her, looking worried.

Maddy pretended not to notice. She wished she could tell Rachel how awful she felt – but then again, Rachel should know without having to ask. A *real* friend would.

But all she cares about now is being Clara, thought Maddy angrily, swinging as hard as she could. Deep down, she knew that she wasn't being fair . . . but she didn't care.

With things so awkward now between her and Rachel, spending time with Ollie was the only thing that cheered Maddy up. She had made a stage for the little cat out of an old cereal box and a red T-shirt, and watched in delight as he strutted about

on it, acting out bits of plays for her.

"*Marry Freddie – ha!*" he intoned, striking a pose with a flourish. There was a pause. "That's the end," he muttered to Maddy out of the side of his mouth, still holding his pose. "You may applaud now."

Maddy clapped wildly. She had

been surprised that a play with such
a dull-sounding name as *Pygmalion*
could be so funny – and Ollie had
been brilliant, acting out all the parts!

The little tabby purred with delight,
inclining his head in a bow. "Thank
you . . . oh, so kind . . . thank you . . ."
he murmured.

Greykin and Nibs sat together in the
"audience". As usual, the two ceramic
cats were touching, which made the
feline magic stronger. Glancing at
them, Maddy thought that Greykin
looked amused, and Nibs rather
grumpy.

She stifled a
giggle. She had
a feeling that the
matter-of-fact Nibs
probably found

Ollie's extravagant ways a bit hard to take!

"Ollie, tell me more about the Aladdin Theatre," she said eagerly, propping her elbows on the desk. "Where was it? Why were you and the other cats there?"

The cat's amber eyes took on a dreamy, faraway gaze. "Ah, the Aladdin! It was the most beautiful theatre imaginable. Especially the

curtain. Red velvet is traditional, you know, but *so* ordinary. So I used a bit of – er, persuasion, and they changed it to midnight blue instead." He beamed at her. "I think blue is much more dignified, don't you?"

"Definitely," said Maddy, holding back a smile at the thought of Ollie using his magic powers to change the curtain colour. "But, Ollie, why—?"

She jumped as her mother came into

the room. On the cereal box, Ollie immediately became smooth ceramic once more.

Mum laughed when she saw him. "What are you doing? Having a show with your cats?"

Maddy's cheeks blazed. "Sort of."

Her mother's expression was thoughtful. "Speaking of shows, shouldn't you be practising for *The Nutcracker* more? I'm sure we could clear a space in the lounge for you to dance in if you wanted."

Maddy shook her head. "No, that's OK."

Mum shrugged, one hand resting on the doorjamb. "All right,

it's up to you. I just wanted to tell you that we're going out to dinner tonight – be ready in about half an hour, OK?"

After Mum had left, Maddy made a face. She felt less like practising now than she ever had. She was only performing in group scenes anyway. She could do those in her sleep!

But as the time for the performance of *The Nutcracker* drew closer, Madame Dumont seemed to disagree. More and more often now, she was telling Maddy off for not concentrating. "You must tighten things up, *ma petite*," she scolded. "Your footwork is becoming very sloppy."

They were now practising at the
Civic Auditorium, on a giant stage
with rows and rows of empty seats
in the audience. "Yes, Madame,"
mumbled Maddy, her cheeks flushing.

It didn't seem fair when she had
always done so well at ballet – and
Rachel hadn't been told off once! The
feline charm continued to work its
magic, and her dancing was smooth
and confident.

*I wish I could tell her why she's
doing so well*, thought Maddy sulkily,
looking away as Rachel tried to catch
her eye.

Then, a week before the
performance, Snow Bradley arrived to
begin practising with them.

Though Maddy knew it was silly,
she'd been half expecting Snow to

turn up in one of her amazing ballet outfits – the white feathered one from *Swan Lake*, or the blue one with ribbons from *Romeo and Juliet*. Instead, she came through the stage door of the Civic Auditorium wearing jeans and a jumper like anyone else.

"Brr, it's cold!" she exclaimed cheerfully, taking off her coat. Her famous pale hair was pulled back in a ponytail, and her eyes were green and sparkling. "Has Madame been working you all hard? She certainly did *me* when I was your age."

Mumbling a reply with the other girls, Maddy stared at the jean-clad woman in wonder. It seemed unbelievable that this was really Snow Bradley!

But then Snow got changed, and came out onto the stage wearing a pale blue practice leotard, with white tights and a filmy white skirt. Standing in the wings with the other mouse minions, Maddy watched raptly as she went through the Sugarplum Fairy's dance.

She made it look so easy! Her leaps were like flying. Rachel was *so* lucky, to be right there on stage with her for the whole ballet – and to actually get to dance with her as well!

Rachel was standing in place on stage, looking as awestruck as the rest of them. In fact . . . Maddy looked more closely at her, wondering whether Rachel was about to lose her

nerve again. Ollie was in Maddy's
bag, back in the changing room.
Could she use the cat magic with him
so far away?

A nasty little voice inside her head
said, *Well, if I can't, it's not* my *fault.
And then everyone would see that
Rachel's not that great after all.*

Her heart pounded at the terrible,
wonderful thought. The beat in
the music came. Snow turned
towards Rachel, hands out. Rachel
hesitated . . . and then lifted her chin
and began to dance.

Maddy let out a breath, half relieved
and half disappointed as Rachel
twirled about the stage with Snow.
Oh, she'd give anything to dance with
Snow herself, just once! The famous
ballerina was so beautiful – and you

120

could tell that she was really nice too.

Maddy looked on wistfully as Snow smiled at Rachel during a pause in the rehearsals. Then she stiffened as Snow's voice carried to the wings: "You have a lot of talent, Rachel. Have you thought of going to ballet summer school next year?"

Rachel's cheeks turned pink. "No, what's that?" she asked shyly.

"It's an intensive programme for gifted young dancers," explained

Snow. "You'd have to audition for it, but I'm sure that wouldn't be a problem for you."

Ballet summer school? Tears pricked at Maddy's eyes. That should be *her*, not Rachel!

She watched in a daze as the ballet continued, with the dancers acting out Clara's adventures in the snowy wonderland. *I can't cry here*, she told herself, clenching her fists tightly. *I just can't!*

Suddenly Maddy came back to herself with a start. The other mouse minions had all left and were halfway out onto the stage. She'd missed her cue!

Chapter Seven

There was a gap in the group of mouse minions where Maddy was supposed to be. Running out on stage, she quickly got into position, stumbling as she tried to catch up with the others.

Suddenly she found herself on her own. She had gone in the wrong direction! Maddy almost fell as she tried to correct herself, and then she was alone *again*, with the other mouse minions moving off downstage.

"Stop, stop!" called Madame's voice. There was an awkward silence as the other dancers came to a halt. Maddy couldn't look at anyone. Her face was on fire. Oh, *why* did this have to happen in front of Snow?

Leaving her seat in the front row, Madame came up onto the stage.

Feline Charm

"This just won't do!" she scolded Maddy. "I've spoken to you several times already, *ma petite*. You must pay attention to what you're doing, or else you won't be able to perform in the show."

"I'm sorry," whispered Maddy. "I – I'll do better, I promise."

Madame shook her head. "See that you do," she said. "You have talent, Maddy, but that's not enough if you won't practise. You should try to be more like Rachel. She always works hard – and see what results she gets!"

"Yes, Madame," Maddy mumbled. She felt as if red-hot coals were sizzling inside her. Be more like Rachel, when Rachel couldn't even dance without the help of feline magic!

Her teacher patted her shoulder. "I know you can do it, Maddy. Now, again, everyone – from the mouse minions' entrance."

After the rehearsal was finally over, the girls in Maddy's ballet class went back to the children's changing room together, chatting eagerly about Snow. "Isn't she wonderful?" sighed Poppy. "Rachel, you're *so* lucky."

"She isn't lucky at all," teased Sue, nudging Rachel with her arm. "You heard Madame – she works really, really hard!"

Rachel grimaced, and gave Maddy a worried glance. "I wish Madame hadn't said that," she whispered, going over and squeezing her arm. "Are you OK?"

126

Feline Charm

"I'm fine." Maddy shrugged. She pulled her hair from its ponytail and shook it out. "Why wouldn't I be?"

Rachel blinked in surprise as she put her glasses on. "Well – because Madame was awfully hard on you, that's why. I think she was really unfair, Maddy, telling you off in front of everyone like that."

Ha – I just bet *you do!* thought Maddy. Rachel had probably loved hearing her get scolded – it meant that *she* got to be the star in front of Snow. "What were you and Snow talking about, anyway?" she asked pointedly.

Rachel looked uncomfortable.
"Um . . . nothing much."

"Really?" Maddy's voice trembled.
"Well, that's funny – because *I*
thought I heard her say something
about a special ballet summer school."

Rachel's ears turned red. "Oh, that,"
she said weakly.

"Yes, *that*," said Maddy. The other
girls had gone silent, watching them.
"Weren't you going to tell me, then?"

"Tell you what?" protested Rachel.
"Nothing's definite yet. I might not
even get in."

"Oh, so you're going to try, are
you?" burst out Maddy. She couldn't
explain why this seemed so unfair, but
it did. A month ago Rachel couldn't
dance without freezing up, and now
she and *Snow Bradley* were having

cosy little chats together about ballet summer school!

"Maddy, what's *wrong* with you?" Rachel's blue eyes were bright with tears. "You've been horrible to me ever since I got Clara! Can't you be just a little bit happy for me?"

"I *am* happy for you!" Maddy cried.

"Why, if it weren't for me—" She stopped abruptly.

Rachel looked as if Maddy had slapped her. "If it weren't for you, what?"

"Yeah, Maddy, what are you talking about?" demanded Poppy with a scowl.

"Nothing!" Maddy flung on her clothes over her tights and leotard. "It's just – it's just that I've given you loads of help with your ballet, Rachel, and—"

Rachel's mouth dropped open. "*What?* Are you saying *that's* why I got Clara – because you helped me?"

"No, of course not!" snapped Maddy, snatching up her bag. She wished she could take Ollie out and wave him under Rachel's nose! But

everyone was already staring at her as
if she'd lost her mind.

"Maddy, what are you *on* about?"
asked Sue, looking bewildered. "First
you say it *is* because of you that
Rachel got to be Clara, and now you
say it's not—"

"I don't know!" shouted Maddy,
stamping her foot. "Just – just leave
me alone, all of you!" She
ran blindly out of the
changing room.

Her mother hadn't
arrived to pick her up
yet. Maddy waited
near the stage door,
trying not to cry. She
knew that she had
behaved very badly
to Rachel . . . but at the

131

same time, it had been something of a relief to finally let her feelings out.

She heard the other girls approaching, and ducked hurriedly behind a vending machine. "Honestly, Rachel, don't worry about it," Poppy was saying. "She's so jealous she can hardly see straight, that's *her* problem!"

Maddy felt sick as she realized they were talking about her. She pressed against the vending machine, straining to hear.

"Yes, and it's really selfish of her," put in Sue. "You're supposed to be her best friend."

"Some best friend," said Rachel bitterly. "I think I'm better off without one!" And then they were gone, with the stage door banging shut behind them.

Maddy's thoughts were spinning as she stepped slowly out into the open again. She *wasn't* jealous of Rachel – how dare they say that! She just knew how unfair it was that everyone thought she was so wonderful, that was all.

A tiny voice inside her whispered that it was true what Madame had said. Rachel had always worked much harder than Maddy, and now that she wasn't nervous any more, her talent shone through. If she, Maddy, worked just as hard—

She pushed the thought away crossly. Ballet had always come easily to her. Madame wouldn't even be thinking that she should work harder now if it weren't for Rachel showing her up!

Glancing around to make sure no one was watching, Maddy took Ollie out of her bag. The little cat stayed ceramic, nestling coolly in her palm. "Oh, Ollie," she whispered, pressing him to her cheek. "I didn't know this was going to be so hard! What am I going to do?"

Ollie's painted amber eyes met hers. There was no response. Finally, with a

sigh, Maddy put him away again and
sat down to wait for her mother.
Tactfully Ollie didn't say anything
about the row once Maddy got home
again. Instead he talked some more
about his life at the Aladdin Theatre,
distracting Maddy with
funny stories.

"I remember once
when we were
working with
GBS," he said,
perched on the
cereal-box stage.
"I was in the stage manager's pocket
as usual (he liked to keep me there,
along with his tobacco), and—"

"Wait – what's GBS?" interrupted
Maddy. "You mean, like . . . in
a car?"

Ollie twitched his whiskers in distaste. "What? No, no, *GBS* – George Bernard Shaw. He wrote that play, *Pygmalion*, and he was *such* a dramatic man himself – he had a great mane of thick white hair, and a flowing beard, and he was over six foot tall! And when he spoke, he . . ."

Maddy almost forgot her hurt feelings as Ollie chatted on. It felt so strange, though, not to be sharing this with Rachel. Her friend had been involved with the cats right from the very start, and was wild to know their history.

Remembering this, Maddy waited for a break in the little cat's story and said, "Ollie, when was all this?"

"Oh, long ago," he said comfortably. He leaped down from

the box with a tiny *thump*. "It seems like yesterday, though."

"Yes, but *when*? And where was the Aladdin Theatre? Was it in London?"

Instead of answering, Ollie prowled over to the pot of pens and markers where Maddy kept the eyebrow pencil. Rising up on his hind legs, he snagged it neatly with his paws and pulled it out.

"Would you be a dear?" he said,

pushing it across the desk towards her. "I can feel a slight tangle on my tummy."

Maddy shook her head with a smile as she began to groom the little cat with the eyebrow brush. She was beginning to suspect that it was no coincidence that Ollie never answered her questions!

In the week that followed, things felt ten times worse than before. For one thing, Rachel wasn't speaking to her. Though this wasn't too bad at school, where Maddy had other friends, it was really dreadful at rehearsal . . . because no one else there was speaking to her, either.

Pretending that she didn't care, Maddy concentrated on her dancing.

Maybe Snow Bradley would notice her, and then the famous ballerina would suggest that she too should go to the special ballet summer school!

But no matter how hard Maddy tried, Snow didn't seem to see her. No wonder, thought Maddy glumly as she sat in the changing room on the night of the final dress rehearsal. She was just one of a dozen mouse minions, with nothing to make her stand out. Why *should* Snow notice her?

She grimaced at the papier-mâché

mouse head she had
to wear. Behind her,
Rachel was laughing
with the other girls
and twirling in a
brightly coloured
party frock. She
looked very pretty,
with her long blonde
hair loose around her
shoulders.

*Snow would notice me if I were
Clara*, thought Maddy, propping her
chin on her hand. It really wasn't
fair, when she was working so much
harder now.

Suddenly Maddy remembered
one of the stories Ollie had told
her – about an actor who'd been so
determined to act in one of the plays

at the Aladdin that he'd haunted the stage door day and night, until finally the director gave him a chance.

"An actor must make his own opportunities!" Ollie had declared, swishing his bushy tail about. "Lady Luck smiles on those who take chances."

A sudden idea popped into Maddy's head. She was the understudy for Clara. Could *she* make her own opportunity somehow? Maddy stared at Rachel in the mirror. It would be so easy – oh, but she *couldn't*; it would be a terrible thing to do!

But the idea was like a determined bee, buzzing and buzzing at her. She bit her lip, wavering.

Was it really *so* horrible? It would only be for this last dress rehearsal, so that Snow could see Maddy dance as Clara. Rachel would still get to be Clara in front of the audience on Saturday night. What harm could it do?

Quickly, before she could talk herself out of it, Maddy closed her eyes. *Cat magic*, she thought, willing it to tingle within her. *Cat magic, please come to me. I need you!*

Chapter Eight

There was a pause . . . and then an electric rush swept through Maddy, tickling her scalp. The magic had arrived!

She opened her eyes and looked at Rachel, still twirling in her party dress. *YOU'VE DONE SOMETHING TO YOUR TOE*, she shouted silently. *YOU REALLY SHOULDN'T DANCE TONIGHT! LET MADDY DANCE INSTEAD!*

Feline Charm

"Oh!" cried Rachel as she staggered.

"Are you all right?" asked Poppy in alarm.

"I – I don't know," said Rachel. She flexed her foot, and winced.

Madame looked up from where she was helping some of the girls with their make-up. "Rachel? What is wrong?"

Rachel shook her head, looking frightened. "I don't know! It's my big toe – it just really hurts all of a sudden."

Guilt pinched Maddy as she saw that Rachel had gone very pale. She bit her lip uncertainly. She hadn't meant to actually *hurt* Rachel – she'd just wanted to make her toe a bit sore!

"Here, let me see," said Madame, striding over to her. She helped Rachel sit down, and eased off her ballet shoe.

"Ow!" cried Rachel as Madame gently moved her toe.

"Hmm," said Madame, looking very serious. "You must have injured it when you were twirling about, *ma petite*. We'll need to tape it, in case it's broken."

Feline Charm

Maddy's throat felt
dry. Suddenly she
realized what a
truly awful thing
she had done.
Hurriedly she called
the cat magic back to
her. As soon as she felt it tingling,
she aimed it at Rachel as hard as she
could.

YOUR TOE'S FINE! she screamed
in her head. *IT'S NEVER FELT
BETTER! IT'S OK FOR YOU TO
DANCE!*

"Oh!" Rachel sat up in surprise.

"What is it?" asked Madame. She
had found the first aid box, and was
just taking out a bandage.

"I – I think I'm OK now!"
exclaimed Rachel, wiggling her toes.

"The pain's gone – it just vanished!"

Madame Dumont's eyebrows drew together. As the other girls watched in anxious silence, she examined Rachel's foot again. "Well – it *seems* all right," she said finally. "Maybe it was just cramp. But I think you'd better not dance on it tonight, just in case. Maddy, can you get ready quickly?"

What? Maddy's jaw dropped as

everyone turned to stare at her. "I – um—"

Rachel looked agonized. "But I'm fine," she cried, jumping up from the chair. "Please let me dance, Madame!"

"No, Rachel," said Madame firmly. "I don't want to take any chances. Hurry, now; let Maddy change into your costume."

"But, Madame, I – I don't think her dress will fit me," stammered Maddy. The other girls were glaring at her as if they blamed her, and the knowledge of how right they were made her feel dizzy with guilt.

"It will fit well enough," said Madame. "Come, we haven't much time!"

It was like being trapped in a

nightmare. Ten minutes later, Maddy found herself standing in the wings, wearing Rachel's frock. Too late she realized that she could have used the magic on Madame again, to make her change her mind – but by then the curtain was rising, sliding up towards the ceiling.

"Maddy! Come *on*," hissed Freya, shoving her in the back.

Maddy quickly danced with the others out onto the lavish Christmas set. Though she wasn't dancing badly, she knew that she wasn't doing her best, either. All she could think of was Rachel, pale with pain.

Poppy was right, she realized miserably. She *had* been jealous, and now her heart ached at what she had done. Oh, she wanted her best friend

back! Somehow she had to make things up to Rachel – but how?

"Relax," whispered Snow in a friendly voice. A tiara glittered in her pale hair, and her pink and white Sugarplum Fairy costume shone like diamonds. "You look like you've got the weight of the world on your shoulders!"

Suddenly it hit Maddy that she was really dancing with Snow Bradley, just like she'd always dreamed of. Despite her worries, a smile spread across her face as they skipped and twirled about the stage together. She was Clara, exploring the winter wonderland with the Sugarplum Fairy – and it was amazing!

The elation didn't last long. All too soon the dress rehearsal was

over, and then Maddy was just
herself again . . . a girl who had done
something horrible to her best friend.

Ollie didn't come to life when Maddy
got home that night. Maddy slowly
got ready for bed, casting sidelong
glances at the little cat as he sat
unmoving on her
chest of drawers.
His expression
was usually
so friendly and
jokey, even in his
ceramic form – but now
his brown striped face looked
quite serious.

Maddy bit her lip. She'd once
promised Greykin that she'd never
use the feline magic when she wasn't

supposed to, and now she had broken that promise. Maybe – maybe the cats wouldn't want to be bonded with her any more, after this. Maybe she had messed everything up for good.

The thought was like a lead weight in her stomach. She swallowed hard and picked Ollie up, feeling his cool smoothness. "*Please* come back to life," she whispered. "I won't do it again, I promise—"

"Have you brushed your teeth yet?" asked Mum, poking her head round the door.

Maddy quickly slipped Ollie into her dressing-gown pocket. "I was just about to."

"Good, and then it's straight to bed." Mum smiled warmly at her. "You must be exhausted after such an

exciting night. Imagine, dancing with Snow Bradley!"

Maddy nodded, trying to look as thrilled as her mother thought she was. She could never explain that the rehearsal had been awful as well as exciting . . . or that Rachel's hurt toe had actually been her fault.

At the thought of what her mother would say if she knew, Maddy felt worse than ever. She was dismally brushing her teeth when she felt a tiny scrabbling in her dressing-gown pocket.

Ollie! Quickly she spat out the toothpaste and wiped her mouth with a towel. "You came back!" she whispered.

Climbing out of her pocket, Ollie leaped nimbly onto the side of the basin. "I've told you before, my dear – you don't get rid of me that easily."

He sat on the rim of the soap dish and peered around the bathroom. "I

see that the number of beauty potions you humans use hasn't decreased any," he commented. "Ah, *vanity, vanity.*"

Maddy thought the little cat was a fine one to talk about vanity, but she let the remark pass. "Ollie, I – I'm really sorry about what I did," she said anxiously. "I won't do it again, I promise."

He sighed, and didn't reply for a moment. "I know you're sorry," he said finally. "And you're certainly not the first human to misuse the powers."

"I'm not?" Somehow this had never occurred to Maddy. It made her feel slightly better.

Ollie gave a shudder. "With human nature what it is? Of course not! And at least you tried to put things right."

157

He fell silent, regarding her with his amber eyes. "But I must warn you, Maddy – if we cats ever feel that you really can't be trusted with your powers, then the magic will vanish."

"That won't ever happen!" gasped Maddy in alarm. "I promise, Ollie. I'll never use the magic when I'm not supposed to again – never!"

"Good," purred Ollie. He swished his thick tail back and forth. "In that case, we'll say no more about it. Now, tell me *all* about dancing with Snow. I want to hear every detail!"

"Rachel, can I talk to you?" Maddy asked shyly. It was the next morning before school, and she'd been hanging around the playground for what seemed like ages, waiting for her friend to arrive.

Rachel peered at her coldly through her glasses. "What do you want?"

Taking a deep breath, Maddy blurted out, "I'm sorry for acting so stupidly. I was jealous, because you got Clara and I didn't, and – and I'm really sorry. Can we please be friends again? I've missed you!"

Rachel's expression had softened as Maddy spoke. "I *knew* that was

it!" she cried, drawing Maddy over to their special place under the slide. "Oh, Maddy, why didn't you say so earlier? I kept asking and asking you what was wrong!"

"I know," said Maddy, feeling sheepish. "I didn't want to tell you – I felt like I should be happy for you. I mean, I *am*," she added hastily. "But . . . well, you know."

Rachel nodded sympathetically. "It must have been really awful for you. I know I wouldn't have liked it very much if *I* was supposed to get Clara, and you got it instead."

Relief rushed through Maddy like a bubbling brook. Rachel was the best

friend in the entire world! "Well, Ollie
says the magic doesn't make mistakes
like that, so I really *wasn't* supposed
to get—"

She stopped with a gulp. Rachel
was staring at her. "Who's Ollie?" she
asked.

"Er . . ." Maddy swallowed.

Rachel clutched her arm. "He's the
third cat, isn't he? He *did* come to life
– I knew it!"

"Well . . . yes," admitted Maddy
reluctantly. *How* could she have
been so stupid? "I didn't tell you,
because . . . um . . ." She trailed off,
wondering what on earth she could say.

Rachel waved this aside. "It's
because you were jealous, wasn't it?
Because I'd just danced really well
for the first time. Never mind that –

what's he like? What's the problem this time?"

Something in Rachel's confident tone irritated Maddy. She needn't just *assume* that Maddy had been so jealous of her right from the start! "You, actually," she snapped.

Rachel's eyes grew wide. *"Me?"*

Maddy could have bitten her tongue off the moment she said it. "Well, no, not *you* exactly," she faltered. "It was more like – you know, you were really nervous, and it was holding you back, so . . . um . . ."

A deep frown had appeared between Rachel's eyebrows. *"What?"* she demanded, propping her hands on her hips.

"Well . . . that's it, really," said Maddy, shifting her weight. "I mean . . . that was the problem. You were so nervous that you couldn't dance very well, so – so Ollie and I calmed you down a bit."

Rachel stared at her without saying anything. Maddy hesitated, and decided that she'd better come clean about the rest of it too. "And when you hurt your toe . . . well, that was me as well," she confessed in a small voice. "I'm really sorry, Rachel. I only wanted to make it feel a tiny bit sore so that—"

"Right, so it was all because of *you*, was it?" interrupted Rachel fiercely. "I got Clara because of you, and I hurt my toe because of you, and—"

Maddy blinked. "What? No, I just meant—"

"Well, I don't believe you, Maddy Lloyd!" broke in Rachel, her voice shaking. "I've worked really, really hard, you know, and you're just jealous because now I'm better at ballet than you are. And I think it's really mean of you to lie about it!"

"I am *not* lying," protested Maddy as the bell rang. Her cheeks felt hot. Rachel needn't throw it in her face that she was the better dancer! "Rachel, listen—"

But Rachel had already stalked off towards the school doors, her blonde hair swinging furiously across her back.

Chapter Nine

That night Maddy lay awake for a long time, angrily replaying the scene with Rachel. "I can't believe she called me a liar," she whispered to Ollie. "And I've been trying to *help* her!"

"Don't be too hard on her," advised Ollie softly. He was curled up in his usual spot on her pillow, no larger than a mouse. "Sometimes the truth hurts, you know. Why, the actors at

the Aladdin used to get terribly down
if they got bad reviews."

Though she knew that the little cat
was probably right, Rachel's reaction
continued to rankle with Maddy
over the next few days. *Well, she
needn't worry*, she thought crossly as
she climbed into her mouse minion
costume on opening night. *I shan't
bother helping her out again!*

It didn't look as if Rachel would
need her to. She was standing on
the other side of the changing room

laughing with Poppy and the others, her cheeks already bright with make-up.

"I'm glad your toe's OK now," said Poppy cheerfully. "It was weird how it got better so suddenly, wasn't it? One minute you practically couldn't walk, and the next, you're fine!"

"No weirder than how she suddenly turned into an amazing dancer." Freya laughed and nudged Rachel's arm.

Rachel started to reply and then stopped, frowning.

A look crossed her face that Maddy had seen a hundred times before – her scientific mind was working something out.

Suddenly she looked across the room at Maddy, who quickly busied herself with pulling on her grey ballet shoes.

Sue had left the changing room to go to the loo, and now she rushed back in, pink-cheeked with excitement. "Oh my gosh, there are so many *people* out there!" she squealed. "I just peeped out through the curtain, and there must be thousands!"

Rachel sat down on one of the chairs with a *thump*. "Th-thousands?"

"Only nine hundred and twenty," corrected Poppy. "That's how many seats there are. But I heard we're completely sold out!"

"Everyone's here to see Snow – and you, Rachel," said Freya.

"Yes, our rising star!" Sue laughed.

Rachel didn't say anything.

168

Feline Charm

Sneaking a look across the room again, Maddy saw that she had gone very pale.

Madame poked her head in. She was looking very glamorous, in a long purple dress and sparkly earrings. "Is everyone ready? It's almost time, girls – take your places!" she said, and disappeared again.

Rachel hung back as the others started filing out of the changing room. "I have to talk with you," she hissed, grabbing Maddy's arm. "It – it *was* you, wasn't it? You weren't lying at all – you've been doing

magic on me all along."

"Of course I wasn't lying," said
Maddy icily, shaking her off.

Rachel gulped. She really did look
very strange, Maddy noticed uneasily
– her face under her make-up was
chalk-white. "Are you OK?" she
asked.

Rachel shook her head. "No, I – oh,

Maddy, I can't do it!" she gasped. "It was only because of you that I could ever do it in the first place, and now – now there are *nine hundred and twenty people* out there!"

"It wasn't because of me that you could *dance*," protested Maddy. "You did that yourself. I only—"

"No, it was, it was!" insisted Rachel wildly. "Maddy, you have to do the magic on me again, or else I won't be any good! I'll go back to being just as awful as I was before—"

"Girls!" Madame was back again, motioning quickly with her hand. "Rachel, hurry – the show begins in five minutes."

Rachel swallowed hard and followed, casting a despairing glance at Maddy over her shoulder.

Maddy trailed after her, her
thoughts spinning. Should she use
the magic on Rachel again or not?
The situation somehow seemed very
different now that Rachel *knew* about
the feline spell. It wouldn't help her
confidence any if she thought that
magic was the only reason she could
dance well!

They reached the wings. Maddy
could hear the low murmur of the
crowd as she hesitated, trying to
decide what to do.

"Maddy, *please*," whispered Rachel.
Even in the shadowy light, Maddy
could see that she was close to tears.
"We've only got a few minutes – I
have to have the magic again, or else
I'm going to be rubbish, I just know
it—"

"What's wrong?" broke in a voice. Maddy caught her breath. Snow Bradley stood beside them in her pink and white Sugarplum Fairy costume, looking more beautiful than ever.

"Um – Rachel's nervous," Maddy explained shyly. "She doesn't think she's going to dance very well."

Snow gave a short, shaky laugh. "Well, that makes two of us. I'm pretty nervous too."

Maddy stared at her in surprise. Rachel's eyes went wide. "*You?*" she gasped. "But why would *you* be nervous?"

"Because I'm human?" suggested Snow dryly. "Rachel, I get terrible stage fright before every single show I do. I was just ill, as a matter of fact."

Rachel's mouth fell open. She seemed lost for words.

"Here, feel my hand," continued Snow. She clutched Rachel's fingers with her own, and Rachel gazed down at them in wonder.

"You're *cold*," she breathed.

"Yes, and I can't stop shaking, either." Snow crossed her arms tightly over her chest. "Because I just *know* that I'm going to be completely awful when I go out there."

"But – but you're
Snow Bradley!"
spluttered Rachel.
"You couldn't
be awful if you
tried!"

Snow made a face. "Well, it's still
the way I feel! So I do understand
why you're scared, Rachel. I am too."

There was a pause. Rachel
swallowed hard. "But – how can
you go on, then?" she whispered.
"Honestly, Snow, I – I feel like I'm
going to forget every move I ever
knew."

"Because I know a secret," said
Snow. She gave Rachel a little smile.
"And do you know what that secret
is?"

Rachel shook her head mutely. In

the orchestra pit, Maddy could hear
the musicians rustling their sheet
music, getting ready to begin.

Snow dipped her fair head close to
Rachel's. "The secret," she said softly,
"is that I've danced this ballet before
– and so I know I can do it again."

Rachel's shoulders straightened
slightly as she stared at her.

"No matter what my head is telling

me, I *can* do this," continued Snow.
She tapped Rachel's nose. "Because
I've danced this ballet perfectly dozens
of times now – and so have you."

The music began. "Go on,"
whispered Snow, squeezing Rachel's
shoulder. "You'll be fine."

"It's time, girls, it's time!" hissed
Madame.

There was a hush as the curtain
rose in a great *swish* of velvet.
Rachel took a deep breath – and then
danced out onto the stage with the
other girls. Maddy leaned against the
concrete wall, smiling. Even without
cat magic, her friend was dancing
perfectly . . . just as Snow had said
she would.

The famous ballerina was still
standing beside Maddy. "By the

way, I meant to tell you before," she whispered. "You're a good dancer too, Maddy – you've got a lot of natural talent. You should have a word with Madame about the ballet summer school. If you keep working hard, you might get in."

"Thank you!" breathed Maddy. "I – I will."

She watched with shining eyes as Snow slipped away from the wings to talk to some of the adult dancers. Snow thought she had talent! If she kept working hard, she might get into the ballet summer school!

And that's just what I'm going to do, Maddy promised herself. She stared out at the stage with shining eyes. Starting that very night, she was going to work as hard as Rachel ever

179

had. Maybe she was only a mouse minion, but she'd be the best mouse minion there ever was!

There was a party after the performance, with the dancers and guests all mingling together, talking and laughing. Maddy wore her grey mouse costume and carried her papier-mâché mask under one arm. She felt fizzy with happiness. Why, being a mouse minion had actually been *fun* – and the audience had even applauded! "Well done, sweetie – you were brilliant!" said Maddy's mum, catching her up in a hug.

Maddy giggled. "You probably couldn't even tell which one I was."

Her father tugged her ponytail with a grin. "*All* the mice were brilliant, so you must have been as well."

"And you were wonderful too, Rachel," said Maddy's mother warmly. "Your parents must be so proud."

"Oh, we are," said Rachel's mother, squeezing her daughter's shoulders. Rachel beamed, looking as excited as Maddy felt. She was still in her Clara nightgown, but now with her glasses perched on her nose.

As their parents started chatting, Rachel turned to Maddy. "Um – I was really a numpty, wasn't I?" she whispered sheepishly. "I'm sorry I got so cross when you tried to tell me about the magic, Maddy. I – I was just afraid that my dancing was all down to that, and that maybe I'm not very good after all."

Maddy almost choked on the fairy cake she was eating. "But you are! The magic just stopped you being so nervous – you did the rest yourself."

"I know that now," said Rachel with a grin. "Thanks, Maddy – a bit of confidence to get me going was just what I needed."

Maddy thought how funny it was. Rachel had needed more confidence, and she had needed less! Dancing had always come so easily to her that she'd never thought she had to practise much . . . but now she knew better.

She told Rachel what Snow had said

to her about ballet summer school,
and her friend's face lit up.

"*Really?* Wouldn't it be great if we
got to go together?"

"It would be *amazing*." Maddy
linked her arm through Rachel's.
Going to ballet summer school with
her best friend would be a hundred
times more fun than going alone – *if*
she got in herself.

But somehow Maddy had a feeling

that she would. She gazed across the
crowded room at Snow Bradley, and
smiled. Whenever she looked at her
poster of Snow now, she'd remember
dancing with her . . . and Snow's
whispered words in the wings.

"I still can't believe that *I* was the
problem," said Rachel, shaking her
head. She glanced over her shoulder
at their parents, and lowered her
voice. "Maddy, did you bring Ollie?
Could I meet him, do you think?"

Maddy fetched her bag, and she
and Rachel stood in the corner near a
giant potted plant, half hidden from
view. Rachel held her breath, hardly
moving as Maddy started to undo the
zip – and then both girls jumped when
Maddy's mother appeared.

"There you are!" she said, jingling

her keys. "Come on, Mad, we need to leave now."

The two girls exchanged agonized glances. "Couldn't we just—" started Maddy, clutching her bag.

"Sorry, sweetie, we need to get home in time for the babysitter." Mum put a hand on Maddy's back, drawing her away from the corner. "Bye, Rachel – we'll see you soon."

"Bye, Rache," echoed Maddy glumly. They both knew that now the problem was solved, Ollie would be leaving soon – that very night, probably. "Um . . . next time, I guess."

Rachel nodded, and tried to smile. "Yeah . . . next time."

"Ah, yes . . . ooh, lovely . . . yes, there, right there . . ." Ollie lay on

his back, purring blissfully as Maddy
groomed him with the tiny brush one
last time. It was very late at night,
and apart from the two of them, the
house was asleep. Only Maddy's
nightlight was on, casting shadows
around the room.

Finally Ollie got to his feet with a

sigh. "Lovely," he said, gazing at his reflection in the mirror on Maddy's chest of drawers. "You know, I think that brush makes my fur even fluffier than usual, don't you?"

"Definitely," said Maddy softly, stroking his tiny head with her finger.

The excitement of the ballet had faded now, leaving her with a sad ache in her throat. Oh, she couldn't bear to say goodbye! She'd had Ollie with her for longer than any of the other cats – and he'd been such a

188

good friend to her when things were
so awkward with Rachel.

"I – I guess you have to leave
soon," she said hesitantly, hoping
against hope that Ollie would say no,
as he had done once before.

But this time the little cat nodded.
"Yes, I'm afraid so. Thank you for all
you've done, Maddy – I know that
it wasn't always easy for you." He
curled his tail warmly about her little
finger.

"That's OK," said Maddy. Scenes
from the past few weeks flashed
through her mind: using her power
on Jack, Ollie acting out *Pygmalion*
for her, dancing with Snow Bradley.
There had been some difficult
moments too, of course – but she
knew that she'd never forget this

time with Ollie, not for as long as
she lived.

She turned her hand over, and the
little tabby hopped onto it, snuggling
into her palm. Maddy rubbed his silky
fur against her cheek. "I'll miss you,"
she murmured.

"Don't worry, I'll be back soon," he
purred. "And it's been most enjoyable
– I must say, I've never had my very
own stage before! Even the Aladdin
pales a bit in comparison with that."

Maddy smiled as she remembered
all the stories he had told her. "Ollie,"
she whispered, "you never did tell me
where the theatre was, or—"

"I'm afraid it's time for me to go
now," he interrupted gently, tickling her
nose with his whiskers. "Would you
take me back to the others, please?"

Even through her sadness, Maddy felt a flicker of amusement. Naturally he still wasn't going to tell her!

Slowly she carried Ollie over to her desk and put him down. He strolled across to the little stage, his bushy tail waving with every step. Maddy had placed Greykin and Nibs on it, and the two ceramic cats sat waiting for him.

Leaping up onto the stage, Ollie took his place beside them and bowed his head. "*Parting is such sweet sorrow*, Maddy," he said softly.

"I know." Her voice caught as she struggled against tears. She stroked Ollie's back one last time. He rubbed his tiny head against her finger . . . and then arranged himself so that his paws were entwined with Greykin's.

"Goodbye," whispered Maddy, hugging herself.

"*Au revoir.*" Ollie's amber eyes gleamed. "Oh, and by the way . . . it was in London. The West End." He winked at her as a shimmer passed through him.

A wide smile spread across Maddy's face. "Thank you!" she breathed.

Suddenly she realized something, and lurched forward. "Ollie, wait! Which of you will be coming to life next?" But it was too late; Ollie was ceramic again, frozen in place.

Maddy let out her breath. She'd

just have to wait and find out, she supposed. And in a way, it didn't really matter – she loved all three of the cats. Tenderly she ran her hand over the little set.

"Goodbye for now," she whispered. "And whoever's going to be next . . . I can hardly wait to see you again!"

THE END

Don't miss
Pocket Cats: *Paw Power*

When Maddy buys three tiny ceramic cats at an antique market, she knows they're special. But it's not until she gets them home that she realizes just how special they are—when one of them *comes to life!* Greykin explains that the Pocket Cats are there to help Maddy, and she and Greykin have a tricky problem to solve: there's a new girl in school who's being picked on by the class bully. Will a little bit of magic and a lot of courage be enough to stop the scariest girl in school?

Don't miss Maddy's next adventure!
Pocket Cats: *Shadow Magic*

Maddy can't wait to get to know Nibs, the second Pocket Cat to come to life! But there's a problem to be solved, and it doesn't take long for Maddy and Nibs to figure out who needs their help. Maddy's cousin Chloe is having trouble settling into her new school; she's so miserable that she's decided to run away. Can Maddy and Nibs use their Shadow Magic to stop her?